Disney's MICKEY MOUSE CLUBHOUSE

LOOK BEFORE YOU LEAP!

By Sheila Sweeny Higginson

Illustrated by the Disney Storybook Artists

PaRragon

Bath • New York • Singapore • Hong Kong • Cologne • Delhi • Melbourne

Mickey and Goofy were enjoying a quiet game of chess. Just as Mickey was about to make a move, something soared through the window and landed right in the middle of the chessboard.

"What was that?" Mickey asked.
The two friends looked carefully at something that
looked right back at them. It was green. It had webbed feet.
It said, "Ribbit, ribbit."

It was a frog – a very jumpy frog. Goofy tried to grab it. *PLOP!* The frog leaped out of Goofy's hands and right onto the silly switch. The room began to spin around. Mickey tried to grab the frog, but it leaped right towards the . . .

. . . kitchen sink. ***KERPLUNK!***
"You really should look before you leap!" Mickey said to the frog.
"What are we going to do about this big puddle?" Goofy asked.
"Oh, Toodles!" Mickey called. "We need some Mouseketools –
right now!"

"The mop is the right tool for this job," said Mickey. "Thanks, Toodles!" All of Mickey's hard work made Goofy hungry. He decided to make lunch. Just then, the frog took a giant leap right towards . . .

. . . Goofy's sandwich. *SQUISH!*

"Stop!" Mickey cried as Goofy was about to take a bite.
"You really should look before you leap," Goofy said to
the frog. "And I should look before I bite!"

Goofy carried the frog outside.

"Hold on tight," Mickey said. "He's pretty slippery."

"I have him. . . I have him. . . *OOPS!* I don't have him!"

Goofy yelped as the frog leaped right towards . . .

. . . Daisy's painting! **SPLAT!**

"You should look before you leap!" Daisy said as the paint splattered everywhere. "Now my painting – and my clothes – are a mess."

"Hey there, little friend," Mickey said to the frog. "Slow down!"
But it was too late. The frog leaped out from behind Daisy's painting and headed straight towards . . .

. . . Mickey's bicycle. **BOING!** He zoomed down the road, holding tightly to the handlebars. He was heading straight for a cliff.

"Oh, no!" Goofy shouted.

"Oh, Toodles!" yelled Mickey. "We need you!"

"The lasso is the right tool for this job," said Mickey. "Thanks, Toodles!"
Mickey and Goofy carefully pulled the bicycle back from the edge of the cliff.

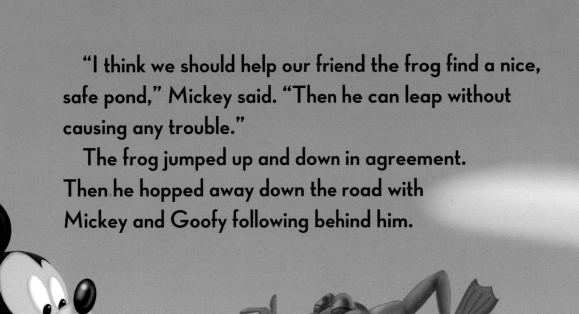

"I think we should help our friend the frog find a nice, safe pond," Mickey said. "Then he can leap without causing any trouble."

The frog jumped up and down in agreement. Then he hopped away down the road with Mickey and Goofy following behind him.

The frog stopped hopping right in front of the pizzeria.
Slowly, Mickey and Goofy crept up behind him.
"We've got to get him before he leaps!" Mickey whispered.
But it was too late. Just as Mickey reached for him, the frog
leaped right onto a . . .

. . . pizza. *SLOSH!*

"You should look before you leap!" shouted the man behind the counter, as tomato sauce dripped off the pizza. The frog stopped for a moment to lick himself off. Then he hopped down Main Street, heading right towards Minnie and Pluto.

"Maybe Minnie and Pluto can help us catch our frog friend and take him to a nice pond," Mickey shouted. But the frog had other ideas. He took a great big leap and landed right inside . . .

. . . the goldfish bowl. **SPLASH!** The big wave made the
goldfish fly right out. Minnie gently put the goldfish back into its bowl.
   "I don't know if we'll ever find a pond for froggie. We need some
help!" Goofy sighed.
   "Oh, Toodles!" Mickey called.

"The net is the right tool for this job," said Mickey.
At last, they held the frog safely in the net.
   "He seems sad," Goofy said.
   "I think you're right, Goofy," Mickey agreed.
Then he looked up ahead and saw
something that made him, and the frog, smile.
   "I think we've found just the right place
for you, froggie," Mickey said.

The friends walked quickly down the street towards the fountain. Carefully, Mickey placed the net on the ground and began to lift the frog out. But the frog was impatient. Out he hopped, heading straight for the . . .

. . . fountain. He landed with a
SWOOSH! right next to another frog.
   "Ribbit, ribbit," he said.
   "Ribbit, ribbit," she replied.

"Maybe we didn't find a pond," said Mickey, "but we did find a good place for him to splash and leap."

"We've found the frog a friend, too," noticed Minnie. "And they look very happy to see each other!"

"I think Minnie's goldfish is happy, too!" added Goofy.

Later, while Donald, Minnie and Daisy made dinner,
Mickey and Goofy got back to their game of chess.

"C'mon, Mickey," Goofy said, "you haven't made a move in a long time."

"I know, I know," replied Mickey. "I just want to make sure I look carefully before I leap!"

QUICK QUIZ

Try this quiz to see how much of the story you can remember! Read the sentences and decide if each one is true. If it is, put a tick in the ✔ box. If it is false, put a cross in the ✘ box.

1 Mickey and Goofy are playing a game of snakes and ladders.

✔ ✘

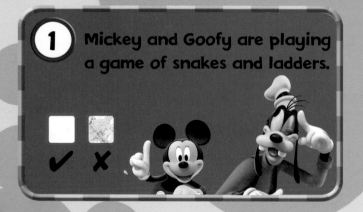

2 The frog leaps onto the silly switch.

✔ ✘

3 Goofy makes a hamburger for his lunch.

✔ ✘

4 The frog leaps onto Donald's painting.

✔ ✘

5 The frog zooms down the road in Mickey's car.

☑  □

✔ ✘

6 Mickey and Goofy use a lasso to save the frog.

 □

✔ ✘

7 The frog leaps into Minnie's goldfish bowl.

 □

✔ ✘

8 Toodles suggests they use a net to catch the frog.

□ □

✔ ✘

9 The fountain is not a good place for the frog.

□ □

✔ ✘

10 Mickey has learned to look carefully before he leaps.

 □

✔ ✘

STICKER FUN!

Use your stickers of Mickey and his friends
to decorate this colourful scene.

Can you find?

A yellow flag ✓

A garden gate ✓

A square tree ✓

Parents' Page

Learning to plan, to make logical choices and to use clues are important skills for pre-schoolers. You can help your child observe and make good choices by playing simple games throughout the day.

1. MATCH AND SORT. Hone observation skills with your child by inviting him or her to join you doing everyday tasks. Your child can match pairs of socks while you do laundry together or sort plastic containers into size order as you cook.

2. PLAY "WHAT IF. . .?" GAMES. Help your child think creatively. What if doors had no knobs? What if cows gave chocolate milk? What if all the crayons in the world were red?

3. MAKE COLLAGES. Keep a box filled with pictures from magazines. Let your child choose various sets of pictures with similarities, such as all the things with wheels, all the red things, all the round things, or all the dogs.

4. HAVE A COLOURFUL DAY. Have fun with your child by designating a "blue" day where everyone in the family wears the colour blue. You could serve some blueberries as a blue-day snack.

5. TALK ABOUT EXPRESSIONS. "Look before you leap" is a common saying that is repeated throughout this book. Help your child understand the meaning of this and other common sayings, such as: "It's a small world"; "Too many cooks spoil the broth"; and "Don't count your chickens before they hatch."

6. PLAY GUESSING GAMES. Take turns using clues with your child to describe what something is: I'm round. I bounce. I'm a ___ (ball!). I fly. I have feathers. I'm a ___ (bird!).